Baggarly

D0466303

From the Library of

Donated by:
Vanessa
Chavez

Immigrant Girl

Becky of Eldridge Street

Immigrant Girl
Becky of Eldridge Street

by **Brett Harvey**

illustrated by **Deborah Kogan Ray**

Holiday House / New York

Library of Congress Cataloging-in-Publication Data

Harvey, Brett.
Immigrant girl.

SUMMARY: Becky, whose family has emigrated from
Russia to avoid being persecuted as Jews, finds
growing up in New York City in 1910 a vivid and
exciting experience.
    [1. Emigration and immigration—Fiction. 2. Jews—
New York (N.Y.)—Fiction. 3. Russian Americans—
Fiction. 4. New York (N.Y.)—Fiction] I. Ray,
Deborah, ill. II. Title.
PZ7.H26747Im 1987   [E]   86-15038
ISBN 0-8234-0638-5

For Perry, Leah, and Nona
B. H.

For the people I grew up with,
who where part of the immigrant
generation.   D. K. R.

My name is Becky Moscowitz, and I live on the Lower East Side of New York. I'm ten years old—as old as the century, Mama says. I live on the fifth floor of 108 Eldridge Street with my Mama and Papa, my brother Max, my sister Dinah, our baby Jacob, our *bubbeh*, who is Papa's mama, and Mama's sister Sonia. We have a boarder named Mischa who lives with us, too. On the bottom of the building is our grocery store.

We came here from Grodno, in Russia, where it was quiet. I knew what would happen every day. Here it is very busy. There are so many people and the streets are crowded and noisy. There is always something to do and something new to see.

We came to America because we are Jews. We wanted to escape the terrible *pogroms* in Russia. I still wake up in the night screaming because I dream that our house is on fire. There was a pogrom in Bialystok, where Mama's family lived. Many Jews were killed and their houses burned. Our *zayde* was shot. Bubbeh would have been, too, but she hid in the cellar. We were terrified that there would be another pogrom. So when Papa's brother, Uncle Ben, wrote us to come to America, Papa and Mama decided we should go.

We have three rooms in our flat. Dinah and I sleep in the parlor with Mama and Papa and the baby. Mischa and Max sleep in the bedroom. Sonia sleeps in the kitchen with Bubbeh. In the evening, it feels like there are twenty people living in the flat instead of nine. It's hard for me to do my homework in the kitchen because there's such a racket. Max and Dinah are fighting, Jacob is fussing, Papa's reading out loud, and Bubbeh is cleaning. Sometimes I sneak out and sit on the fire escape just to be by myself.

In the morning I have a lot to do. Mama and Papa have already gone downstairs to open the store, and Sonia has left for work. First I have to get water from the faucet in the hall. I bring Bubbeh her glass of hot water with lemon. "These old bones can't move without it," she says. I help Dinah get dressed and give Jacob his bottle. Mischa always seems to be in the way while I'm getting breakfast for Dinah and me. We have bread and herring in the morning. After Max empties the ash bin and I sweep the kitchen, we take the baby to Mama and Papa in the store. Then we go to school.

Our school is four blocks away on Rivington Street. It is called Public School 20, and it looks like a castle made of red bricks. It is so big that at first it made me feel as small as a mouse. My teacher, Miss Reilly, smells like roses and has a lace hanky tucked in her sleeve. Miss Reilly says we have to clean our teeth with brushes, and she looks for dirt under our fingernails. I am learning English fast because I don't want to be a "greenie." That's what they call you when you're new in America. I still have trouble mixing up v's and w's. Once some children in my class laughed at me because I said "adwenture." Miss Reilly corrected me. I wanted to crawl under my desk and stay there. My favorite part of school is art class because everyone likes the pictures I draw. I don't have to talk and be afraid of saying something wrong.

After school I take care of Dinah and Jacob. I wrap the baby up, put him in his little cart, and go out on the block. My friends Rachel and Sadie are there too with their baby brothers and sisters. We play jacks and potsies and jump rope. The middle of the street belongs to the boys, but sometimes they let us play ring-a-levio or prisoner's base with them.

Whenever I find a piece of chalk, I make pictures on the pavement. Everyone watches. When the delivery wagons drive over the drawings, my friends yell, "Hey! Get off Becky's pictures!"

My brother Max is a "newsie." Every afternoon he and his friends go uptown to sell newspapers. He gives most of the money he makes to Mama and Papa, but he keeps a little for himself. It makes me boil that I can't go uptown like Max and make my own money even though I'm older than he is. Some girls are newsies, like my friend Pearl. But Mama says she needs me at home.

On Sunday, if Max has any money left over, he takes me to the nickelodeon. We've seen *The Schoolboy's Revenge* and *The Queen of the Ranch* and *Baby Swallows a Nickel.* Max and I could stay all day in the dark, watching the pictures moving on the screen.

Some days I shop for Mama after school. I take her big oilcloth bag and go to Hester Street. The peddlars yell *"Weiberle! Weiberle!* Come by me and get a good *metsiah!"* The carts are piled with peaches and eggs and hats and tin cups and handkerchiefs and bananas and spectacles and shoes and chickens and umbrellas and pots and pans. There's a woman who grinds horseradish and a very old woman who pushes a baby carriage. It has a big pot of beans in it. She calls, *"Bubkes!* Come and get my fresh hot *bubkes!"* I like to buy a pretzel or a roasted sweet potato for three cents.

Every other week I go to the library on West Broadway. At first I couldn't believe I was allowed to take so many books home. I like to visit the library because it's so quiet.

When it rains we stay in the store after school with Mama and Papa. Sometimes Mama and I read my library books together. Mama keeps a dictionary under the counter because she is always trying to learn English words. She says, "If I make a mistake in my English, correct me. Don't worry, I wouldn't be angry." Mama is in charge of the money and Papa is the seller. He tells stories and argues with the customers about politics. Papa is a good storyteller. He can always make people laugh and then they buy things.

My aunt Sonia is seventeen. She works in the Leiserson Shirtwaist
Factory all day. At night she goes to school at the University Settlement.
She's making me a dress trimmed with bits of lace she brought home
from work. Sonia tells me stories about her job. She sews on a machine
in a big room with thirty other girls. Her boss keeps the doors locked so
no one can get out. He won't let her and the other girls talk or hum or
even get a drink of water. When they don't sew fast enough, he yells at
them.

One night Sonia took me to a meeting of the shirtwaist workers. We walked uptown to a big hall in Cooper Square. People were jammed into every corner of the hall. Sonia's friends from the factory were all there. Everybody was talking about going on a strike to make bosses treat them better and pay them more. There were a lot of speeches, and I fell asleep. Sonia woke me because her friend Clara was speaking. I didn't understand what she said, but when she was finished, everyone jumped up and started shouting "Strike! Strike!" Now Sonia wakes up even earlier in the morning to go out on the picket line. Mama says Sonia doesn't have to give her rent money until the strike is over.

My bubbeh is very old and the same size as me. Her face is wrinkled like a walnut shell. She thinks she's strong, but she's not as strong as she thinks she is. She cooks and cleans the house and takes care of Jacob while I'm at school. Bubbeh goes to *shul* every afternoon to pray. I have to help her up the stairs when she comes back. Bubbeh won't learn English. She makes us speak *Yiddish* so that we won't forget it. She says it's her job to make sure we don't get so American that we lose our Jewish faith. Bubbeh and Mama had a big fight when Mama decided to grow her hair and stop wearing her *sheitel*. I was glad because Mama's hair is prettier than her sheitel.

On Thursday night we have our baths and wash our clothes. We want to be clean for *Shabbes* the next day. Mama and I heat water on the stove and pour it into the big washtub. Mama lets Dinah and me get in first. The water is still warm and bubbly instead of gray and cold the way it is at the end. After we've had our baths, we wash our clothes and hang them to dry.

On Friday Bubbeh gets up early to start making the *challah*. When we get home from school, the whole flat smells delicious from the challah baking. We dust and sweep and scrub the parlor and kitchen. Then we black the stove and polish the brass candlesticks Bubbeh brought from Grodno. We have to get everything done fast because we're not supposed to do any work after sunset when Shabbes starts. "Run next door to Mrs. Cohen, Becky, and look at her clock!" Bubbeh keeps telling me.

When the table is set with a white cloth and Bubbeh's candlesticks, Mama *bentsh licht*. Then Papa says *kiddush*, and we sit down to eat. We have roasted chicken and challah and noodle *kugel*. Sometimes there isn't enough money for a chicken, so Bubbeh makes herring stew. But we always have the challah and the white cloth and the candlesticks. It's the only time in the week we all eat together, so everyone talks at once. Usually I'm trying to tell about school, Max and Dinah are teasing Mischa, and Papa and Sonia are getting into an argument about labor unions. Then Bubbeh hits her plate with her fork and shouts *"Shtil!* No arguing at the Shabbes table!"

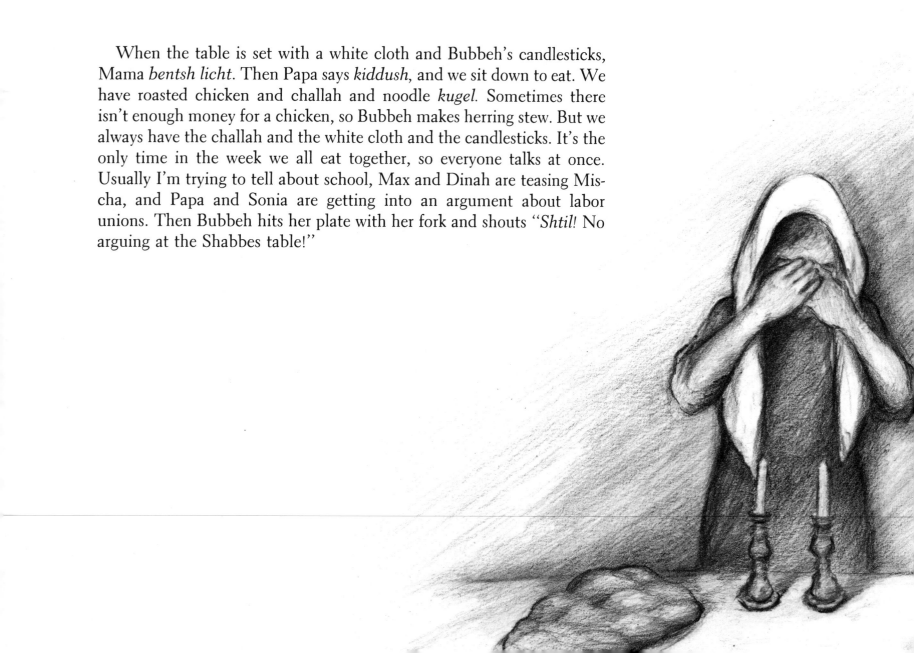

On Saturday we go to shul with Bubbeh. We walk down the street to the Eldridge Street Synagogue. It's packed with people, and noisy and hot. Max and Papa sit with the men. Mama, Bubbeh, Dinah and I and the baby sit with the women. The babies always cry and the little kids fight and run around under the benches and between people's feet. The mamas and bubbehs have to shush everybody. They try to keep the babies quiet with pieces of bread and bananas.

In the summer the sidewalk burns my feet, and the tar in the street bubbles. When the Italian hurdy-gurdy man comes, we girls dance and dance until we almost melt. Then we turn on the hydrant and play in the water to cool off. Every day we have to buy ice from the iceman to keep our food from spoiling. Max and his friends go down to the river in the afternoons to swim. When Max comes back, his skin is so dirty, he has to rinse off under the hydrant.

At night everyone sleeps on the roof and the fire escapes because it's too hot inside. Up on our roof I can see the stars. Sometimes there's a salty breeze from the river. When there's a cloudburst, everybody screams and grabs the babies and blankets and runs inside. But Max and I like to stay and let the rain cool us off. We watch the lightning split the sky over the city.

One Sunday Papa woke us early and said he had a surprise. He was going to take us to a wonderful place. Bubbeh packed hard-boiled eggs and oranges and salami sandwiches in a big basket. Mama and I dressed Dinah and Jacob in their best clothes. Papa took a blanket off the bed and tucked it under his arm. We wondered where we were going.

We rode on the elevated train for the first time. It made me feel dizzy to be on a train so far off the ground. The train was already crowded with people when we got on. Each time it stopped, more families climbed on with their baskets of food. Whenever the train lurched, everyone fell on everyone else, and people screamed. As we looked out the window, the buildings got lower and lower and there were big spaces between them. We began to see more and more grass, and then trees, and then Mama started to cry. I think she was homesick for Grodno.

Papa called the place the Bronx Park. There was a big field with trees that made me think of Grodno. Mama and Bubbeh hugged each other and danced on the grass. Papa spread the blanket on the ground, and Bubbeh set the food out on it. She sat down and turned her face up toward the sun. Dinah and Max and I took off our shoes and chased each other. It felt good to run wherever I wanted, with the grass soft and damp under my feet. We ran in bigger and bigger circles until we heard Mama calling, "Not so far! Not so far!" When we looked back it scared us to see her so small and far away, so we ran back. After we ate, Papa let us climb all over him and threw us in the grass. Mama took us on a walk to pick flowers for Bubbeh. Bubbeh made crowns for Dinah and me. We stayed in the Bronx Park until it was almost too dark to see, and then we went home. I didn't want to leave, but Papa promised we'd come back again.

In the spring, as soon as it's warm enough to stop using the stove, Bubbeh opens the windows. She starts getting us ready for *Passover*. We hang our bedclothes outside the windows to air. We scrub the whole flat, because during the winter everything gets covered with black soot from the stove. "Turning the house upside down," Papa calls it. Bubbeh goes through the flat like a wind. If we don't hold on to our favorite things, she sweeps them away or gives them to poorer families.

This year's *seder* was special because it was our first on the East Side. We had so many people in the kitchen, we could hardly squeeze into the room. Uncle Ben and Aunt Hannah and my cousin David came. Sonia brought a friend from work who had no family to go to. Papa even made a special chair for Jacob so that he could sit at the table.

Papa led the seder, but Bubbeh sat next to him to be sure he didn't forget anything. Papa reminded us that Passover is about the Jews who were freed from slavery in Egypt three thousand years ago. He said we were like those Jews because we came from Russia to America to be free.

At seder this year, we talked about how Mama's other sister Mollie would soon be coming from Grodno. Mama and Papa sent her the money to come with her husband Nathan and my cousin Rosie. They will stay with us until they find a flat of their own. Mama says we have to help them get settled. She says to remember how we felt when we first came here. I remember. I will have to show Rosie everything about the East Side. I can't wait to take her to our school and to the nickelodeon and to the Bronx Park. I know she'll like it here.

GLOSSARY

(The words in the glossary are in italics the first time they appear in the text.)

Bentsh licht (BENCH LISHT): to bless the Sabbath candles.
Bubbeh (BUB-eh): grandmother
Bubkes (BUB-kiss): hot, black-eyed beans.
Challah (HAHL-leh): a braided loaf of white bread made for the Sabbath.
Kiddush (KID-dish): the blessing for the Sabbath and holidays, said over wine.
Kugel (KOO-guhl): pudding.
Metsiah (meh-TSEE-eh): a bargain or lucky break.
Passover (PASS-oh-ver): the eight-day spring holiday celebrating freedom and the Jews' escape from slavery in Egypt.
Pogrom (poh-GRUM): an organized massacre of the Jews.
Seder (SAY-der): the ritual meal of Passover.
Shabbes (SHAH-biss): the Sabbath, which lasts from sunset on Friday to sunset on Saturday.
Sheitel (SHAY-tul): a wig worn by Orthodox Eastern European women after they are married.
Shtil (SHTIL): quiet.
Shul (SHUHL): synagogue.
Weiberle (VEE-ber-lee): ladies.
Yiddish (YID-dish): the language of Eastern European Jews.
Zayde (ZAY-deh): grandfather.